# QUICK
# AND
# QUIRKY

# QUICK AND QUIRKY

## SHORT STORIES WITH QUIPS!

**Fred Onymouse**

Illustrations by Ann Onymouse

Matador
9 Priory Business Park,
Wistow Road, Kibworth Beauchamp,
Leicestershire. LE8 0RX
Tel: 0116 279 2299
Email: books@troubador.co.uk
Web: www.troubador.co.uk/matador
Twitter: @matadorbooks


ISBN 9781788039123

British Library Cataloguing in Publication Data.
A catalogue record for this book is available from the British Library.

Printed and bound in the UK by TJ International, Padstow, Cornwall
Typeset in 13pt Gill Sans by Troubador Publishing Ltd, Leicester, UK

Matador is an imprint of Troubador Publishing Ltd

MIX
Paper from
responsible sources
FSC® C013056

Short stories for anyone who might enjoy them — a degree is by no means a necessity, but a SoH might help... and PoS definitely would!

SoH = Sense of Humour
PoS = Pinch of Salt

# AUTHOR

Fred left secondary school at 14, without any GCE or A-Levels.

He found a job in the warehouse of a small firm, and worked there for ten years. Then he went to work in the warehouse of a supermarket, for nearly 30 years.

He has only been writing creatively for the past two years, before that he scarcely wrote at all... but Ann (his wife) thinks he has a colloquial quirky humour – of a 'je ne sais quoi' ingenious kind!

Fred has also written the lyrics for Ann's children's rhyming short stories book: *The Conjurer's Mouse*.

Fred          Ann

# CONTENTS

# BUTTONS

As we all know, there are millions of buttons in the world – all different sizes and shapes: some with six or four holes, and some with two holes. There are even some very ancient ones, with just *one* hole – but not so many of those. This is about some **extra special** buttons!

There were two sisters in the North of England, Elsie and Doris, who were both button-mad. They had a room in their house, completely covered with buttons. Buttons were stuck to the walls… the ceiling… everywhere there were buttons!

Each week on a Wednesday, they opened their doors to anyone who was interested in seeing their display. Women mostly would come in, and pay fifty pence to browse through them.

Now, the sisters had some **extra special** buttons in their collection, which were worth a lot of money. They kept these buttons in a metal box, fastened to the wall with bolts, as a safety measure; and although they tried to keep it a secret, word got around.

It wasn't long before a gang of boys wanted to get their

hands on the **extra special** buttons. Every time they came to see the display, they kept looking at the box. Would it be possible to rip, or more likely, drag it off the wall?

The gang leader, a bit of a boaster, said, 'I could easily get that box off the wall.' 'How?' asked one of his mates.

'I'll get a sledgehammer. That will shift it… if I give it a good whack.'

'How, are you going to get into the house?' another of his mates queried.

'I don't know yet, but I'm working on it,' said the leader. 'You could do some thinking too!'

The boys went home, pondering on how they could get into the house.

Elsie and Doris decided to have a holiday, and they locked the door of the room, with the button box in it. They had their house burglar alarm set, so that the buttons would be safe, and the button box was alarm-wired inside.

When the gang heard that the sisters were going away, they jumped for joy. 'Good,' they said, 'now we can get the **extra special buttons**!'

They got a sledgehammer, and tried to get into the

house. They had to be very quiet, so as not to disturb the neighbours, and they then decided, 'We'll go through the skylight window, if we can get it open.'

They pushed and pulled each other up, but they couldn't open that either. They didn't want to break the glass, as it would make a noise and would wake the neighbours.

The gang worked at attempts to open the skylight for half-an-hour. In the end, they had to give up for the night. They would be back tomorrow, with another plan on how to get into the house!

The next night the boys were back with some shovels. After about an hour, they managed to dig a tunnel through the garden, and were able to squeeze themselves into the cellar – but they didn't know that the house was burglar alarmed – and one of the boys set the alarm off! They quickly covered up the cellar opening, and crawled back down the tunnel.

When the police arrived, they puzzled at first, as to how someone could get into the house and set off the alarm. They managed to contact Elsie and Doris, about resetting it, and returned to their station.

The third night the gang came back again, and after removing the covered opening, they crawled into the house. This time they were ready for the alarm, and managed to disengage it. They forced the lock on the button room door, being used to that. And they were able to carry on with the job in hand, trying to get the box off the wall.

They'd brought some bolt cutters and succeeded in loosening the box, but it still wouldn't come off the wall! So all the boys tugged, and tried to twist it. It wouldn't budge any further!
In the end the leader said, 'Right there is only one thing for it. We'll have to chance it, and smash it off the wall!'
The leader grabbed the sledgehammer, and gave the box one almighty **BASH!**

Finally, the box crashed down to the floor.

**'GREAT!'** the boys yelled, at last they would get the **special buttons.**

'We might be seen carrying it home – I'll have to open it,' the leader said. He *hit* and *bashed* it with the sledgehammer. Then he asked, 'who'd like a go now?'

By this time the police had arrived, and stood watching the boys trying to open the box. The noise also woke up the neighbours, who came to see what was going on. They couldn't believe that the gang got into the house, without being heard.

The police interrupted the *hitting* and *bashing*. 'You're coming along with us! We're arresting and charging you, for breaking and entering, and wilful damage.'

Just as the police were leaving with the gang, Elsie and Doris came back to their house. Elsie cried, 'What's been going on here?'

The police said, 'These boys broke in, and have dragged your box off the wall. Now they've been trying to get into it!'

Doris said, 'I'll open it, and show you what you want to see.' She opened the box with a key from her pocket, and out fell masses of **peanuts.** They said to the boys, 'EVER BEEN

HAD? *WE KNEW SOMEONE WAS AFTER THE EXTRA SPECIAL BUTTONS – SO WE TOOK THEM WITH US AND HERE THEY ARE!'*

Now, in case you're wondering what happened to the gang, Elsie and Doris decided not to press charges. Instead of buttons, the boys set off home with their pockets full of peanuts, but they'd been exceptionally lucky, don't you think?

*But that isn't quite the end of the matter...*

Elsie and Doris were just enjoying their early cup of tea next morning, when they heard a lot of banging. They went down to the cellar, and a head poked up through the floor. 'You're not back already!' Doris gasped.

'We've come to block up the hole we made,' the leader told her. 'Sorry, ma'am – no offence intended, but anyone could get in.'

There was more banging, then silence. Elsie and Doris watched as the gang walked out of the garden gate. The leader made the thumbs up sign, and the others waved. The sisters waved back and Doris said, 'We should have given them a cup of tea.'

But just to be on the **SAFE** side, they put their extra special buttons in a large tea caddy in the kitchen cupboard, behind a jar of marmalade, a bag of flour and a big box of sticky dried fruit… seeing as the alarm was no use at all…

The box had an extra lock fitted. It was nailed and bolted firmly back on the wall, and then it was filled with… *now that would be saying…*

Well, you can't be too careful, with **extra special buttons**!

# tIt FoR tAt

There were two elderly men – both keen gardeners. They were neighbours, and you'd think this would make for happiness, wouldn't you?

It didn't!

When Mr Smith bought a **gnome** for his garden, Mr Brown bought a bigger one.

That was only the start of it.

When Mr Brown bought a **fountain** for his goldfish pond, Mr Smith bought a bigger one. (The goldfish must have felt cramped, but that wasn't the point, was it?)

When Mr Smith bought a **greenhouse** for his garden, Mr Brown bought a bigger one.

How would it ever fit in? (But that was beside the point, wasn't it… somehow it was squeezed in. It had to be!)

Then Mr Smith bought a **big tomcat**, which somehow preferred to do its doings in Mr Brown's garden.

So Mr Brown said to his wife, 'What about a nice big tomcat dear? It would keep the mice away.'

'No thank you, my sweet!' his wife replied briskly. 'I don't like cats and there aren't any mice to keep away.'

Mr Brown tried not to swear. Then he suddenly thought **moles** make much the same mess on a lawn…

'How about a mole, dear… you'd really love a mole. They're no trouble at all, not to us anyway.' Mr Brown wasn't giving up.

'A **mole**,' his wife repeated in surprise, 'you mean the garden kind?'

'Of course, dear,' Mr Brown smiled, 'I wouldn't suggest anything **nasty**, you know that!'

**'The kind of mole which lives underground?'** his wife still looked amazed.

'Yes dear,' Mr Brown said patiently, 'they're sweet little things, just like mice…' he saw his wife grimacing so he hurried on, 'but you don't have to clean up after them… goodness no, moles are terribly **clean** animals… you once had a moleskin coat remember?'

That rang an uncomfortable bell in Mrs Brown's mind. 'Yes, poor little thing… we'd better have a mole.'

'Good, that's agreed then. I think you'll love it, dear.' **He** certainly would. Their mole would burrow down and into the garden next door — he'd see to that!

The only snag was **where would he buy their mole?**

Was it even legal to own a wild animal? There didn't seem to be many moles, if any, about. He'd have to find one and catch it himself. **Where?** He'd never seen one recently — in fact, apart from nature books, he'd never seen one at all…

He'd have to make a mechanical one… No, he'd buy one in the local bazaar shop — they sold **everything,** didn't they?

It would really look better if his wife bought it… neighbours might talk, if they saw him buying a toy mole… but somehow, he couldn't ask her, she might change her mind!

He went down to the local bazaar shop that morning. They didn't have mechanical moles, only monsters — but you wound it up and it moved by itself. Not ideal, though somehow it might travel down a tunnel… push its way up into the lawn next door… make a small mountain of grassy mud… and travel back again, before it got caught!

Mrs Brown came into the garden, as her husband began to dig the tunnel. 'WHAT ON EARTH ARE YOU DOING, DEAR?' she asked loudly.

It disheartened Mr Brown then he had a brilliant idea!

'I've been thinking hard,' he said, 'how would you like a dog, dear? I mean **Alsatians** are very lovable aren't they.'

His wife looked astonished. 'But you always said a dog would ruin the garden!'

'Yes, well I've changed my mind,' Mr Brown mumbled.

'I wouldn't mind a miniature dachshund,' his wife said, smiling. 'Now, they *really* are cute.'

*And they bark, or rather, **snap**... it would drive everyone mad, including me,* Mr Brown thought silently.

Then he smiled. Yes, that's what they'd buy... yes! Yes! Oh Yes!

'Of course, my dear,' he said, 'I'll get us one straight away.'

He went down to the local pet shop, and ordered a miniature dachshund.

Mr Brown collected it next day. 'Let's call it *Hitler*,' he suggested mildly to his wife.

**'Hitler?'** his wife was shocked. 'Personally, I think she's simply **sweet**... we'll call her **Lucky.** I just feel she's going to bring us lots of **luck**!' Mrs Brown hugged her husband, who looked somewhat dazed.

'Yes dear,' he said, hugging her back. 'Yes, I like it. What an ideal name.' Except he'd thought he'd bought a *he*, not a *she!*

And would this miniature female dachshund bring them any **luck** at all?

13

That afternoon the Smith's **tomcat** squeezed through the hedge to do his doings as usual.

*'Go for him!'* Mr Brown breathed.

Lucky didn't go for him. No, she started to bark… a rather high-pitched **yap**… and she didn't stop, as the tomcat stared back in surprise.

'I can't stand this,' Mr Brown wailed, just as Mr Smith was doing the same thing.

'But it's **because** of our cat,' Mrs Smith told him sensibly. 'I always said we shouldn't let our **Tom** go into their garden… I mean look at the mess he makes there!'

'Those Browns **deserve** it,' Mr Smith replied between his teeth.

So, what happened in the end – was it all out **WAR** perhaps?

No! The pets decided the matter for themselves. **Tom**, the Smith's cat, fell in love with **Lucky**, the Brown's dog... and Lucky showed Tom *discrete* places in both gardens, where they could do their doings. Tom showed Lucky how to bark softly, so it almost sounded like *purring*!

Competition between the neighbours was abandoned, as you can't have a perfect garden, if you also have a pet. The Smiths and the Browns enjoy the sunshine, while drinking their afternoon tea together... or chatting over the hedge.

*Now if one has a neighbour, it's better to be a friend –*
*Or goodness only knows where it all might end!*
*In many cases, **NASTILY** – or at the least **SNAPPILY** –*
*Though in this case, I'm glad to say, the answer was **HAPPILY!***

# COUNCILLOR

Wilmot Walmesly was new to his job of Sunnerset's Councillor. He'd won his seat by a very narrow majority indeed. In fact, being an extremely modest man, he was sure he never would! And he very nearly didn't! He had 2,000 votes, and Jogger Jaggersnout (nicknamed *Joker*) had 1,999 votes – it was as close as that!

Now Wilmot had one over-sized disadvantage in the field of local politics. He was EXTREMELY **SHY**, as well as

extremely modest… whereas Joker, his closest opponent, was EXTREMELY **EXTROVERT** – what you might describe as a *BIGHEAD* – if one held opposing views.

At the local events (never missing one), Joker turned up in full force. He flirted with the women, and joked noisily with the men. It was extremely ODD that he hadn't managed to clinch matters this time. In fact, it was downright CRAZY!

Wilmot was making his unobtrusive way round town one day, when he heard a group gossiping. 'You know what I think?' one woman said loudly, 'I think there was a mistake in the **counting**!' 'That's strange,' a man said, nodding, 'that's just what I said to my wife!' 'I said the same,' yet another man put in, 'I thought someone can't count.' 'I did,' the first woman burst in, 'it was a miscount, anyone could see that!' 'Or a vote was dropped on the floor!' a second woman added. 'Yes, or ten were!' the first woman finished triumphantly.

Wilmot felt faint with shock, and hurried into Sainsbury's to hide! How was he going to handle this unbearable situation… not to mention these *unbearable* people!

He bought himself a large bar of chocolate – sat down outside, in a corner of the seat where those of low means, low repute or low anything else gathered, and ate his chocolate bar. Then he felt much better, and was suddenly aware of the man beside him.

He was old, very old, had a long very bushy white beard, shaggy white eyebrows, and a twinkle in his blue eyes!

'Are you Wilmot what's-his-name?' the old fellow asked.

'Yes sir,' Wilmot replied politely, 'that's me, the very same.' At least someone knew who he was, from his picture!

'I voted for you,' the old fellow said. 'I used to vote for Joker – but I changed my mind. That bighead promised the best this, that and the other! Did I get any of it? Not a bean.'

'Well…' Wilmot began, trying to remember exactly what he'd promised.

'You didn't promise anything,' the old fellow told him. 'So, I said to myself, this fellow Will W… whatever – at least he's **honest!** I like that in a council lad, so I voted for you.'

Wilmot beamed at the old fellow. 'I think your vote swung the counts for me!'

'Of course they did,' the old fellow nodded wisely. 'I wrote out ten just to be on the safe side.'

Wilmot went a shade of bluish-white, and nearly fell off the seat.

'But the girl stopped me. She said one would do, so I had

to trust her, didn't I?' the old fellow smiled his big Sunnerset smile.

'Thank you,' Wilmot smiled back and put his arm round the old fellow. 'You've made my day! What can I do for you?'

'I'd like to come to a dinner at your mansion some time,' the old fellow replied. 'I'm free most nights.'

'What about tonight… around six o'clock?' Wilmot asked.

Now at six o'clock that night, Wilmot was holding a very important dinner for all the most important people in his new constituency… with one new addition – a very unimportant person who was a respectable, slightly disreputable old fellow. HOW WOULD IT ALL WORK OUT?

At six o'clock all the most important people arrived. Wilmot hovered in the background, ready to serve sherry – or in some cases, cocktails. He'd shaken everyone by the hand, and everyone had drifted off to talk to everyone else… when the bell rang … **and Joker walked in.** *Who had invited him? No one!* But it didn't seem to matter. Everyone at once swarmed round **Joker** and there was extremely **NOISY LAUGHTER!** And now everyone was drifting into the dining-room of their own accord, while Wilmot wondered what could possibly go **WRONG worse than what already was!**

Everyone sat down and Wilmot stood up to say, 'I'm highly honoured that you could all come, **JJJJogger Jaggersnout** included,' then he sank down drained as driftwood – wishing he could float away. He knew what everyone would talk about, *local politics, what they wanted, and* (in loud whispers) *what went wrong!* After all, it was most likely many, if not all, had voted for Joker...

'We'd much rather have had **YOU** as our Councillor,' one large, very drunk woman was nearly shouting to Joker, who was sitting next to her. 'I mean you've always... **OWWWWWWWW...** *take your hand off my KNEE...'* she jumped out of her chair and nearly fell over. While everyone stared at Joker, nearly as shocked as she was.

'I ddddidn't touch you,' Joker stammered. 'Would I do that to you?'

And this seemed to enflame the woman even more. 'Are you *insulting* me?' she demanded furiously. 'Aren't I **young enough** for you?'

The whole matter was getting out of hand, and the local head of police reluctantly left his starter shrimp cocktail, and walked over. 'Now, now,' he said, trying to laugh, but not too much, 'I'm sure Jogger never meant to touch you...'

Well, that was the last straw.

The large woman smoothed her tight-fitting dress, and marched out saying loudly, 'I'M GOING HOME! I WILL NEVER VOTE FOR JOGGER AGAIN!'

Jogger excused himself, with a false genial smile and hurried out too. Then everyone else sat down to enjoy their dinner.

After the meal and coffee in the lounge, everyone went home, assuring Wilmot that they were **SO** thankful he was their Councillor – and they would **DEFINITELY** VOTE FOR HIM NEXT TIME.

Wilmot completely drained, stumbled back into the dining room and… ***stared in shocked delight.*** An old fellow was eating his starter, at the place of honour, next to his own place at the head of the table!

'Sorry, I'm a bit late,' the old fellow began, 'you see, I was kind of tired when I got here… so I lay down under the

table and had a snooze. Then suddenly this leg kept nudging my bad shoulder… more and more.'

Wilmot nodded his head.

'Well, I'm ninety-six,' the old fellow went on, 'I can't have that, can I? So I gave her a tiny shove, like this...' the pepper-pot flew across the table!

'I understand **absolutely**,' Wilmot said and winked.

The old fellow smiled his wide Sunnerset smile, and Wilmot smiled equally widely back.

Some smiles say something, others do not.
In this case, both of the smiles said a lot!

# HOLIDAY ELEPHANTS

This is the true story of holiday elephants... about a coach load of people who went on holiday to Devon, and one *particular* couple. Altogether there were about forty passengers; and after being picked up from their local pick-up points, they were all taken to Reading services, for the changeover to their holiday coach.

They arrived at their hotel at four o'clock. They then checked in, and went to their rooms.

By coming at the beginning of December, the hotel was celebrating Christmas early, as advertised. They all arrived on Monday, while **Christmas Day** would be on the Wednesday. Everyone had a *Christmassy* meal the night they arrived, to get in the *mood*.

The following day they all went on an outing to another part of Devon, and got back in time for their evening meal.

The particular couple, mentioned before, was Brian and his wife Carol. They had a nice room but on the second night, Brian was ill. It may have been the seafood he'd had for lunch, and was rather partial to... he was being sick continually, and then kept going to the toilet. The people up above banged on the ceiling – but he couldn't help a few odd noises. He was unable to get to bed until about four o'clock in the morning!

As a result of going to bed late, they overslept, and were told they were too late for breakfast…

After a nice day going around the seaside resort (Brian having avoided seafood), they went up to their room. Then Carol heard a **drilling** sound, which went on and on. They went down to the Christmassy hotel reception, and told them about it.

A man in a paper hat went up to their room and said, 'Yes, I can hear the sound!' He told them, he would investigate and see what was causing it.

This he did – and found it was coming from the cellar – but he told Brian and Carol that he couldn't do anything until the morning. He said if they went back to reception, they might be offered another room.

Brian and Carol went back to the Christmassy reception, and the receptionist (who was enjoying a Christmassy drink) offered them another room: number fifty-five. They went to no. fifty-five – but the sound was still there!
The receptionist glared at the sight of them. 'I have only one more room available: number sixty-seven.' They went

to have a look at no. sixty-seven, and although they could hear the sound, it wasn't quite as loud – so they decided to take it, and moved all their belongings into that room.

By the time they had changed rooms, it was too late to go downstairs for their **Christmas dinner** and they weren't in the mood for the entertainment, so they decided to stay in their room. They were just dropping off to sleep, when they were woken by drunken noises and slamming doors. Again they slept in and missed breakfast next morning!

Well, it was their last night in the hotel and it was time to pack up. It only took them about an hour to do, as the rest would have to be done before breakfast. Then they climbed into bed, hoping for a quieter night at last, with only the slight drilling sound.

But the couple in the room above them, made so much **noise** it was just like **elephants** banging and crashing across the ceiling: **thump, thump, thump** went their feet on the floor – backwards and forwards – up and down. **Crash Bang Wallop!** The **noise** was **HORRENDOUS!** This went on until twelve o'clock at night, and then the **ELEPHANTS** put the television on at twelve-thirty!

The television noise went on to past one-thirty. Then

believe it or not, there were **TRUMPETING** *noises,*

*as well as* **thumps,** and a most *peculiar* smell. Brian and Carol tried to bang on the ceiling by throwing things up, but this made the **TRUMPETING** *noises* **WORSE** – so they got out of bed and made themselves a cup of tea.

The **NOISE** was still going on at two o'clock. When it stopped at last, Brian and Carol were so wide awake, having drunk *numerous* cups of tea and coffee to soothe their ragged nerves – they scarcely slept a wink.

In the morning, the noise started up again, but not quite as bad as the night before. Brian and Carol went down to breakfast, looking like they felt; and they left the hotel at nine-thirty, to go to their changeover point at Reading, where they would get their coach home. They arrived home at five o'clock.

## BUT WHAT A HOLIDAY!

First, they'd had the boiler drilling sound – though it was nothing compared to the noise up above. Who'd have thought a hotel in Devon might have **ELEPHANTS** staying there…

*I mean, you don't often get elephants in the room above you, when you're trying to enjoy a Christmas holiday, do you?*

# MAGIC

In Norfolk, there was a man who loved doing magical tricks. His name was Ernie, and he lived in a small flat with his wife, Jackie. They had one big sadness in their happy lives… they couldn't have children of their own – but Ernie loved to use his talent for entertaining children.

In fact, he was so professional that he became well-known, and was frequently invited to children's parties. Then one afternoon, he was asked by a parent, 'Why don't you become a full-time magician, Ernie? You could make a living that way!' 'Yes, maybe… I would love to, you know,' Ernie replied seriously. He hadn't thought of it before and never charged for his magician's shows – but suddenly, it seemed an exciting idea!

Throughout the next couple of weeks, Ernie discovered how to do even more tricks, and then he contacted a magician's club. He started to ask questions about being a full-time magician.

The directors of the club asked Ernie to go on stage, and show all his tricks to the committee. They were impressed by his skill, and told him, 'Yes, we'll enrol you as one of us!' They gave him a certificate, which he took home and framed.

Ernie's first official magician's job was at an old people's home. He did a number of tricks for them, and made them all laugh. Many said the show had done them the world of good. It was in the local newspaper – and word spread further afield about his magician's shows.

Lots of bookings came in for his services – and his wife, Jackie helped him to keep a record. He had birthday parties, an engagement party, a wedding where he would entertain the children, during the reception... he even had invitations from overseas, he'd become so well-known for his deft movements and pleasant manner. However, he turned those down, as he had more than enough already!

Then Jackie's mother was suddenly taken ill. Ernie cancelled many of his shows, so that he could accompany Jackie on hospital visits. It was a very worrying time, and to worry them further – they returned home one night, to find that all Ernie's magician equipment had disappeared.

It seemed to be the last straw, coming at such a time. Ernie was depressed as it was... their money was running low, without his magician's income. His popularity was dwindling, as he'd let so many customers down... and to add to it all, he had a rival magician in the same town. A new man was offering to do the same tricks as Ernie had done.

He read in the local paper: *Ernie Johnson, our popular magician is out of action – but have no fear! Terry Dixon, a new man to these parts, has told me he is more than willing to fill the bill. His phone number is...* Ernie threw the paper in the bin. He knew now, without a doubt, who had stolen his equipment.

Should he tell the police? Wasn't he jumping to conclusions? What if Terry Dixon was innocent – could he himself be had up for **slander?**

Ernie was nearly sick with indecision. Then he knew what he'd do, whatever the outcome... He'd go and see exactly what tricks Terry Dixon was doing.

But he didn't want to worry Jackie, so he'd have to do it alone... He'd torn up the telephone number, but he found it in the bin. Somehow, he managed to make out the numbers. He would phone up Terry Dixon and ask him... though he wasn't sure what!

'Yes, tell me briefly which night you want my services for?' a male voice said impatiently.

Ernie mumbled, 'Are you free tonight?'
There was a noisy laugh. 'You must be joking I'll be at

the *Crown and Tarter* pub tonight – doing my act. Phone again, tomorrow,' the phone was slammed down.

Ernie was speechless and shaking, but he was going along to the *Crown and Tarter* tonight, where he'd performed so often in the past!

He drove Jackie to the hospital, but didn't tell her. She'd only worry and want to come with him. She said, 'What's on your mind, Ernie?' 'Nothing much… I'll tell you later,' Ernie laughed it off.

As he'd come in the car, he decided he wouldn't drink, but settled on a snack. Terry Dixon had arrived, dressed up in black dinner suit, with a pink satin bow tie. He had an infectious cheeky smile, and everyone was smiling at him. Ernie felt like a deceitful spy, which he supposed he was.

It was all just a hunch, after all! He stroked the pub's cat to calm his nerves. Then he looked across at another familiar mate, who had joined noisily in the fun, when he'd done his tricks in the past – but there was no response from there!

The lights were dim enough, but they dimmed further, and Terry began his magician's act. **'GOOD EVENING ALL!'**

The response echoed somewhat drunkenly back.

'Oh dear,' Terry began to sneeze, 'I've got the **sneezes** and lost my hanky… has anyone seen it?'

'What colour?' a man standing nearby, asked.

'Red as wine,' Terry replied, winking. He turned all his pockets inside out, then jerked from the same man's pocket, not just the one hanky, but more and more – a string of them! 'Dear me,' Terry smiled at him, 'have you caught **my sneezes already?** Better buy some tissues!'

Ernie had done a similar act in the past, but he'd always avoided that particular man, who was usually drunk. And true to form, the man looked confused and annoyed, almost as if he would start a fight. Then to add to it all, the pub's parrot flew from his perch, squawking **'ERNIE'S HANKY!'**

Terry soothingly produced a bouquet of paper flowers from behind his back, but instead of **soothing** the drunk, the man spluttered and pushed it away.

**'ERNIES'S FLOWER! ERNIE'S FLOWER!'** the parrot squawked.

Someone muttered, '*Shhhhhhh! You've got it wrong!*' and the manager said crossly, 'Clear off, Duke… get back to your perch, silly old bird!'

But this appeared to goad the parrot, who squawked even louder, **'ERNIE'S HANKY! ERNIE'S FLOWER! SILLY OLD MAN-GER! SILLY OLD MAN-GER!'**

The manager grabbed the barman's towel, and waved it at the bird.

Then another man shouted, 'WHY IS IT ERNIE'S HANKY?'

The parrot perched on Terry's shoulder and shrieked,

# 'THIEF! THIEF! SILLY OLD THIEF!'

Terry lost his cool and swiped at the parrot – but the bird was too quick for him. Instead his hand hit a young woman, who dropped her glass into an elderly man's lap.

'I'm calling the police,' the young woman snapped. 'I came here for entertainment, not a drunken brawl!'

The parrot flew over to Ernie shrieking, 'ERNIE'S HANKY! ERNIE'S FLOWER!' Then he changed it to, 'ERNIE'S PUP-PET!' as the cat dragged the puppet from Terry's bag, 'ERNIE'S HANKY FLOWER PUPPET! ERNIE'S HANKY PUP-PET FLOWER...'

'Could someone shut that parrot up?' Terry gasped, gulping down two whiskeys.

Well, that was the end of the evening's entertainment! The police discovered Ernie's initials on all of the magician's goods. Terry Dixon said he was doing the act on Ernie's behalf, and would share the proceeds – but no one believed that, drunk though quite a few were! The pub gave Ernie compensation, and it all worked out for the best. Ernie bought new equipment, and learnt many much more exciting tricks.

As the old saying goes: Though men be drunk on whiskey or stout… without a doubt, the truth will yet, out!

# CHINA SET

In a small village in Yorkshire, there was a handicapped villager, Norman. He was often helped by Geoff and James, the boys who lived next door; and he decided, one day, that he'd like to give them something for their kindness. He would sell his large collection of china, which he had accumulated over the years, and give them the proceeds.

One morning near Easter, he told the boys he wanted to sell his collection. 'We'll help you,' they replied, not knowing what Norman planned to do with the money raised. Norman said, 'I'm going to hire a room in the men's club down the road.'

The manager of the club agreed that Norman could hire the biggest room for his sale. It was decided that he could have it on the Saturday before Easter, and Easter Monday.

On Good Friday and early Saturday morning, Norman and the boys took some of the china over to the club. They set up as many tables as they could. It was a big job, but by the time ten o'clock came, everything was ready.

The sale got off to a moderate start; but soon more and

more villagers were looking at the china. By six o'clock on Saturday evening, Norman and the boys had sold most of it. They locked the room, and gave the key to the club manager.

Early, on the Monday morning, they took more china over to the club, and collected the key. Everything was ready by ten-thirty, and a number of people came in to buy. Norman, Geoff and James were kept busy.

At about twelve-thirty, Norman decided they needed to have a break. They locked up the room, and had a quick lunch at a café nearby. 'We'll be finished early at this rate,' Norman said, 'I hope the best china goes!'

But when they got back, they had a big shock. A fragile bone china vase lay smashed on the floor! How had it happened? Who would do such a dreadful thing?

Norman had a word with the manager, and asked if anyone else had a key to the room. The manager said, 'No, nobody has had the key recently.' It was a mystery, and Norman began to worry more and more. What if his most expensive china set was broken? Would there be enough money, for both the boys?

The villagers heard about it. 'It's those boys, Geoff and James,' one woman said. 'They're big clumsy hunks, those two. Poor Norman, I feel sorry for him!'

A man nodded his head, 'Clumsy hunks the pair of them!' Then very soon everybody agreed with this verdict – except Norman. He'd heard the rumour spreading down the queue, and was horrified. Soon, he couldn't stand it and shouted, 'SOME CHINA IS BROKEN. WE DON'T KNOW HOW, BUT I'VE DECIDED WE'VE SOLD ENOUGH. MY GOOD FRIENDS, GEOFF AND JAMES, WILL HELP ME PACK UP! SORRY TO DISAPPOINT – THANK YOU FOR COMING!'

'Well! Well!' the same woman muttered. 'But we'll find out who did it… those boys, I bet you!' Just as she finished speaking, pigeon droppings landed on her nose. 'Oh noooooo!' she wailed. 'And they say it's supposed to be lucky!'

'But I'd say it's lucky for Geoff and James,' a young woman put in. 'They're good boys – always helping Norman!'

And the young woman was right. Just at that moment, as Geoff and James helped to pack up, Norman spotted white droppings on his best china… and two pigeons fluttered from under the table. How had they got in, when the door had been locked and the windows were closed? They must have slipped in with the morning queue, flown around in frustration trying to get out, and knocked over the fragile vase.

Well, Norman and the boys had a good laugh. Then the

boys carried the pigeons outside, and Norman decided they'd all done more than enough work. 'I'm giving you half of the takings each,' he said, 'and you're sharing the rest of the china. That'll give you both something to dust!'

After they had packed the remaining china, and given the key back to the manager, they had a slap-up supper at the local pub.

BUT ONE THING, THEY DIDN'T CHOOSE, WAS THE PUB'S MOST POPULAR DISH.

WHAT WAS IT?

WOOD PIGEON PIE!

# BINGO

In Lancashire, there was a Social Club for middle-aged and retired men and women. There were several games going on, but the most popular was **Bingo!**

Bingo was on most nights, so the club was full. It started at 7.30 p.m. in the evening, and ended at 10 o'clock. Most of those playing bingo were women.

There were all sorts of prizes for the **bingo**: table mats, trays, tea towels, and mystery prizes of varying kinds, mainly ornaments; but soon there was a murmur going round, 'I've got enough of those already – without getting more!' 'Not worth winning!'

Toby, the manager, overheard and quickly bought boxes of chocolates, instead.

Then an argument arose over soft or hard-centred chocolates – and what about toffees?

**Could he ever please them all!** Toby decided to buy a selection, and they could choose.

But worse still, women were going to the dentist more

43

often. 'I'll have false teeth, if I keep on winning at this rate!' an older woman moaned loudly. A skinny younger one overheard. 'You can swop your chocolate boxes for my bar any time...' 'NEVER – though I will, when I break the scales!' the older woman replied.

Toby heard all this and thought, *'that shouldn't be too long!'* He was right. Very soon the scales in the Ladies broke down...

And he'd already wondered how their teeth would suffer!

He decided there and then, to start paying money prizes. *But where would the money come from, when sweets were expensive enough!*

Toby lay awake at night, worrying. Then he finally decided: all the people in the club had to fill in a registration form, to show that they were members. They were all given a membership card, and had to show it every time they went to the club. They also had to pay £10 a year, to join – and with so many members, the money soon mounted up.

Then they paid £2 for the bingo every night (and the same for all the other games). The bingo prize money was £20 for a full house; and £1 a line, £3 for two lines. In the second half, the prize money was more; the lines were the same but a full house was £35.

At the end of the bingo, all the winners were very happy – but the losers, as usual, were pretty upset and moaned that they didn't ever win.

Toby said, when the evening was over (as he always did) 'Goodnight to you all, and better luck next time to our losers!' He decided to ignore any more grumbles over prizes or anything else; he had to be sensible and stop trying to please everyone!

The club was going well enough, and Toby breathed evenly again. He was even sleeping better – when he was suddenly called by the **police**… at three o'clock in the morning. The club was on **FIRE!**

The fire brigade was already there, and the police thought the cause of the fire was ARSON.

There was not a lot of fire damage – most of the mess was damp round the toilet areas, from the water used to put the fire out. But the club would be closed for over a week.

The members were becoming impatient – it was taking longer than expected. Then suddenly, it was up and running again, but there was endless ill feeling! Mutterings and whispered hints! *'Still smoking?' 'Better be careful you don't start a fire!' 'Your coat smells of ciggies!' 'Yours smells of fags!' 'Ciggies!' 'Fags!' 'Bad for your health!' 'Watch out yourself!'*

Soon everyone was suspicious, if only mildly, of everyone else! Toby felt uncomfortable – he had a private smoking habit himself. He was constantly washing shirts, and collecting suits from the cleaners!

It seemed the vague sense of suspicion would never stop, until it was interrupted by **another** incident. One very cold night, the police phoned and told Toby they'd found an old tramp, crawling out of a downstairs window! He admitted that he'd been smoking and about a month earlier, he had dropped a cigarette, panicked and left the club in a hurry… that was enough to start the fire! As the place was always checked before closing, the police gathered he'd often ask to use the toilet, and when the **Gents** was being checked, he'd hide in the **Ladies** – usually in the cupboard, with the cleaning equipment in it. As that was damaged the most, it was fairly obvious who had started the fire!

The tramp looked very unwell, so the police called an ambulance and took him to hospital, having warned him never to use the club's toilets again. And a lock was put on the cupboard door.

It was an unfortunate happening, but at least no money had been stolen, and ill feeling about **smoking** among the members stopped!

As time went by, and it was coming up to **Christmas**, Toby said that he had saved some cash and everyone would get a Christmas present, while the bingo prize money would be higher.

Then just a week before Christmas, a hooded man came to the club's entrance. He waved a gun at the receptionist, and demanded the money from the safe.

'You've got a lot in there,' he snarled, 'I heard those women talking!'

'I'm sorry I don't know the code number,' the

receptionist tried to stay calm, 'the boss hasn't given it to me…'

'Get him,' the man snapped, 'and tell him to bring any prize money with him – otherwise someone will get hurt – and no funny business!'

Toby heard the man's raised voice, and sensed something was wrong. He came through to find out what it was all about.

'WHERE'S THE MONEY?' the thief shouted at him.

'It's in the safe,' Toby replied calmly.

The thief snarled, 'You'd better get it or your receptionist will be beaten up. I'll beat you up as well!'

Toby replied, 'Give me five minutes… '

The thief had by now tied up the receptionist and gagged her. 'Hurry up,' he hissed, 'and get me the money!'

Toby bent down to undo the safe. He put in the code and he started to take out the money, and at the same time he managed to grab an old walking stick…

Keeping it behind his back, he handed the thief the money – and whacked his hands as he did so!

The thief, taken by surprise, dropped the gun and the money. And Toby quickly picked them up and locked them in the safe. He called the police on the phone, as the man ran out of the office… Then he heard a **LOUD BELLOW…**

The thief, hearing the police car, had made for the ladies toilet, and knocked over an old tramp, having a quiet smoke. The cleaning cupboard door was unlocked, so the thief darted in there… and the old tramp crawled over and locked him in!

The police arrived as the thief tried to break the door down. He was arrested for attempting to steal the money, having a fire arm, threatening the receptionist, gagging and tying her up, threatening Toby, and knocking over an old tramp!

By now Bill, the caller, wondered what was happening, as Toby had never come in to pay the winners. He continued with the game and told the winners, 'Come and see me afterwards in the office – I'll give you your money there. It will still be in the safe… I guarantee that… *safe and sound…* '

Soon afterwards, when Bill walked into the office, Toby immediately told him about what had happened. The police had taken the thief away, and the receptionist now recovered, had made the tramp a reviving mug of tea.

Well, neither Toby nor Bill mentioned it to the ladies, as they collected their winnings. Somehow, they'd had enough excitements in their bingo club without adding to them… and this had nearly been the last straw!

It was also the last bingo for the year, and they would carry on in the New Year. Toby wished all the players he saw, *a very merry Christmas* and gave them a card with a gift token inside – but it was a very disjointed evening, and the women were aware that something strange had happened… particularly, as they'd noticed the old tramp having tea with the receptionist…

When all the women had gone home, Toby and Bill joined the receptionist and the tramp for mugs of tea – and the receptionist and the tramp were given well-earned cash Christmas presents, the tramp having promised to give up smoking!

NOW, IF YOU RUN A BINGO CLUB KEEP A WALKING STICK IN YOUR SAFE WITH THE MONEY. IF YOU NEED EVEN MORE HELP THAN THAT… AN OLD TRAMP'S YOUR MAN… AND I'M NOT BEING FUNNY!

# tEApotS

Two friends, Jane and Eve, lived together in the Midlands. Over the years they collected **teapots**, all shapes and sizes. Wherever they went, they brought home a teapot. They had a wonderful collection of big, small, miniature, human jokey, animal-shapes, crazy novelty ones and a silver-crested. Altogether, they had about two hundred!

Jane and Eve decided to put all the teapots on show, so they cleared their dining room, and laid them out on tables, shelves, and wherever there was some space. They held a **Teapot Day**, when the local people could come in, and see the teapots.

Much to Jane and Eve's surprise, quite a crowd turned up. Then a stranger came in, and looked at the teapots very closely. He offered the friends, five hundred pounds for the collection. Jane said, 'Sorry, we aren't selling our teapots.' The man smiled and said, 'You don't know me, but my name's Horace Hawkson – I'm an antique collector. I'll up my offer to £700.'

Jane said, 'Sorry, no deal! We really don't want to sell our teapots.' Horace Hawkson was very annoyed. He went off, trying to hide it.

Eve had seen his face and later she said to Jane, 'One way or the other, Horace Hawkson looks like he won't give up!' 'But he's not having our teapots,' Jane replied, 'I don't really trust him – though I don't know why!'

In the morning, Horace Hawkson came back. He asked, 'Can I have another look at your teapots?' He gazed at the teapots then added, 'This time, I'm offering you one thousand pounds for the collection.'

'No!' Jane said firmly, 'I'm sorry but we've told you they're not for sale.' Horace Hawkson nodded curtly and walked out.

Hawkson had only got as far as his car, when he decided to watch the house. About half an hour later, he spotted Jane going outside to do some shopping. He said to himself, 'This is my chance to get their teapots!' He went back to the house, and asked Eve if he could have one last look at them. Eve agreed and let him in.

Hawkson started picking up some of the teapots. Eve said, 'Put them down, you might drop them!'

Hawkson said, 'Why don't you sell them to me, your friend won't know. I'll give you twelve hundred pounds.'

Eve said, 'Jane's already told you they are not for sale!'

This really got to Hawkson, and he lashed out at Eve hitting her in the face. He then hit her in the stomach, and knocked her to the floor. Just as he was going to hit her again, Jane came back and saw what Horace Hawkson had done to her friend. She picked up a broom and started hitting him with it, and he ran out of the house.

Although Horace Hawkson had disappeared, the police said they would keep a look out for him. They told the two friends, if he came back he'd be arrested.

Then Jane called an ambulance to take Eve to hospital, to be checked over. Eve came back from hospital, a bit bruised on the face and round the eyes. They closed the room for a few weeks, so that Eve's injuries could heal.

But Jane and Eve wondered why Horace Hawkson wanted the teapots so much. They contacted a specialist, to find out how much the teapots were worth. The specialist pointed to the crested silver one. 'This is what Horace Hawkson wants — it's unique, very old and valuable.' The specialist added he would come to their house in the morning to check the total value of the teapots.

Next day, the specialist told them he would give them £10,000 if they ever wanted to sell the collection.

A few weeks later Jane and Eve reopened the room where the teapots were, and people came in to see them. Horace Hawkson heard about it; he parked his car behind some bushes so it couldn't be seen, put on a beard, a moustache and dark glasses and walked up to the house.

Using a foreign accent, he said 'I understand you have a **Collection of Teapots** to see.'

Jane said hesitantly, 'Yes, we have.'

'I have come a long way to see these,' the disguised man went on. 'Why don't you sell the teapots? I would be willing to give you twelve... no, fourteen hundred pounds... maybe fifteen...'

The friends shook their heads, and again Jane said they were not selling the teapots.

The disguised man dropped his accent as he swore loudly, and Jane and Eve became suspicious of him. Eve went into the hall and immediately called the police, while Jane stayed in the room with the man. The police got to the house very quickly, and arrested Horace Hawkson.
'What have I done?' he demanded. 'I only came to see the teapots.'
'Take that false beard and moustache off,' a policeman told him. There was a scuffle... the moustache fell onto a duck teapot, the beard dropped onto a human-jokey one, and the top flew off a novelty teapot, which sang, *'Stay! Stay! Don't run away! Time for tea... just you and me!'*
Eve groaned and Jane put her arm around her. 'I'll make us a cuppa, that's just what we need.'

Hawkson was charged with assault. When he went to court, he was jailed for two years.
After about six months, Jane and Eve started to get fed up with the teapots, and rang up the specialist to ask him if

he was still interested in buying them. He said, 'Yes, indeed I am! I'll come over in the morning, and help you to pack them up.'

In the morning, the specialist came and gave Jane and Eve his cheque for ten thousand pounds. All their teapots were sold, and Jane and Eve put the cheque in the bank.

Jane and Eve had some friends in Australia, and decided to have a holiday there. After about six months, they returned back home but they had decided to go and live in Australia. They sold their house and moved there, and both Jane and Eve married and settled down happily.

*Now, if a voice inside you hints of a fight... better be wary, it just might be right!* Jane and Eve were **wary** as they argued with Horace Hawkson – and now they enjoy cups of tea (made from teabags) in the sunshine, while having a good laugh about bogus teapot collectors – and TEAPOTS!

# HORSES

In Yorkshire, there was a man who lived on his own. His name was Barry, and he had a friend whose name was Owen.

Barry had four horses, left to him by his uncle, but he found he had no great interest in owning them. However, he fed them and let them eat the grass in his field; he also put up sheds there, so the horses had somewhere to stay at night, or shelter in during the day, if the weather was bad.

After about a month or so, Barry became more absorbed in his horses. He suddenly decided to see if he could find a racehorse from among the four, enquired about getting a licence to become an owner; and he made Owen his partner.

The racing board sent a man to inspect Barry's yard, and agreed to Barry getting a licence, but said he would have to secure his property. He would also have to get a vet to check the horses to see if there were any ready to race. And if he wanted his horses to be entered for racing, he would have to get jockeys.

Barry got a fence put round his stable yard, so that everything was secure. The vet came and examined the horses, and picked out two which would make suitable racehorses: BLUEBELL and CHESTNUT! Then work started, getting the horses exercised and fit to run.

A couple of weeks later, Barry's licence came through, and he was to be the legal owner. Owen became his trainer, as well as partner, and more serious work had begun!

It was about six months, before his horses were ready to run in a race. Barry and Owen looked through the racing guide, and found a small racecourse in Wetherby. They entered BLUEBELL and CHESTNUT for races, and took them there in a horsebox. BLUEBELL would run in the 2 o'clock and CHESTNUT in the 3.30 p.m. race.

After a nervous start, BLUEBELL finished fourth, and CHESTNUT finished third. Barry and Owen were very pleased. It was also a good beginning for their two jockeys, and they all set off happily for home.

*But on the way, Barry sensed something was wrong at his yard... and the feeling wouldn't go away!* When they got nearer, he saw the yard fence had been dragged down... it was almost as though he'd expected it!

Barry and Owen parked the car and the horse box, and

running into the yard, they found the sheds were empty. The other two horses had gone! Had the horses escaped by themselves, or been stolen? Barry phoned the police, and they said they'd check other stables. But they could be difficult to trace, as Barry had no CCTV.

And finally, nothing came of it. Barry decided, instead of dwelling on it, he'd buy another horse. He called the new horse DAISY – she was smaller than the others, and white! Then it turned out that she didn't enjoy racing. He would only be putting her in for special events, such as dressage.

**One night DAISY disappeared.** Had she run off by herself? The fence was broken, as before.

Or had she been stolen?

Barry was certain that this was the case, but again, the police weren't hopeful of finding her. The stable CCTV had been installed, but it was turned off. And that was odd in itself! Barry's suspicions deepened, though he was too disheartened to follow them through.

He and Owen wearied of horse racing, decided to pack up and retire. They went to the neighbouring farm a few miles away, and Barry asked the farmer if he would be interested in buying his horses, BLUEBELL and CHESTNUT. The farmer came over and they reached a deal.

Then Barry and Owen decided to have a holiday – a cruise on the Queen Mary, and see the world. It would take their mind off their losses.

But on the cruise, after three months abroad, Barry was taken ill. He had somehow caught a tropical virus, and it was touch and go whether he would survive. They managed to get him off the ship, and taken to hospital. He was put in intensive care, while Owen stayed by his side. After weeks in hospital, Barry recovered and he and Owen returned to the ship.

Then the day after the cruise was over, they heard the news from the police: **DAISY HAD BEEN FOUND NEAR THEIR HOME!** It greatly added to Barry's renewed health, and both of the men's happiness. Barry immediately decided they would keep her.

When one evening, the same thieves returned, and tried to steal DAISY, she was more than a match for them both! The damaged CCTV showed their back view, staggering off together.

Now it happened, when Barry was having a check-up at the local hospital, he noticed his two jockeys. He went over to talk to them, but they turned away.

*And it suddenly became clear to Barry!*

They had stolen his other two horses…

While one jockey was in a race at Wetherby, the other had ridden over to the yard, smashed the fence and gone off with the horses! Then he'd returned to the racecourse.

That night, Barry heard on the local news: BLUEBELL and CHESTNUT had been bought from the farmer he'd sold them to.

Barry sighed – the next thing his jockeys would be racing them! He told Owen about it.

But when he went to see DAISY next morning, Barry had the surprise of his life!

Shaking, he read the note pinned inside the shed door: **We thought DAISY might be lonely, so we bought BLUEBELL and CHESTNUT as a present for you.**

**What should he do about it?**

The old saying is: HORSES FOR COURSES, WHICH GOOD FOLKS TEND AND WATER!

While another goes: BAD MEN GET THEIR JUST REWARD, DOING WHAT THEY DIDN'T OUGHTA!

The boys had had their **just reward!** In the local hospital, they had both looked very sorry for themselves – DAISY had seen to that.

*And perhaps they had really changed their ways?*

Barry discovered the jockeys' address from the farmer – then he wrote a note, thanking the boys for the horses, and enclosed a generous cheque.

His favourite three horses were back with him and all was well! But DAISY needed a special friend now, just as humans do. He bought a fine black horse, called DANCER – which turned out to be just the right one for DAISY. Between the two of them, **they could see off anyone up to no good!**

Also, he had a hidden voice alarm attached to the fence

and stables – his own voice saying: **'I knew YOU did it all along!'**

And it was true… he'd known ever since that first race at Wetherby, by intuition… the way owners who love their horses do!

# MIX-UP

Two teenage step-brothers, Barry and Gerald, went train-spotting whenever they were bored. They lived with their grandfather in Southampton, and they'd go to the many platforms in the main station there.

The boys were on holiday for a few weeks and went train-spotting as usual. As they walked through the car park, they had a nasty shock. A van was driven out in such a hurry, it nearly knocked Gerald over. Barry grabbed Gerald, then

quickly jotted the van's number down, in his train-spotting notebook: IOU 900P – though they could hardly forget it!

Gerald was still shaking and instead of train-spotting, they went to the café and had a sandwich and coffee. Their grandfather had said he would give the one with the most train numbers, twenty pounds at the end of the holiday – but Barry could see Gerald had lost interest. 'We'll go to a film instead,' he said.

As they were walking towards the cinema, 'That's the same van,' Gerald gasped.

'We'll follow it,' Barry replied.

'They're up to no good,' Gerald gasped, 'I can't believe they drove so wildly.'

The van was parked by the side of the road, and the driver and another man leapt out. Barry and Gerald followed them.

It seemed the men had gone into a jewellery shop. They ran out in seconds, holding carrier bags.

As the boys tried to phone the police, a police car drove up. Barry and Gerald wanted to stop the policemen, but they ran into the jeweller's shop. 'We'll have to wait,' Barry said, 'we've got to tell them about the van!'

When the police came out, Gerald blurted, 'If that was a smash and grab, we know who did it. Their van number is …' but the policemen raced past.

'I suppose they're hoping to catch the men,' Barry said. 'They've probably seen them on CCTV.'

The boys were about to go, when a man who had been standing close by, walked up. 'I'm a plain clothes detective,' he said and produced his warrant. 'Could you give me the van number? It might be just what we need...'

'IOU 900P,' the boys chorused.

'Excellent!' the detective said, smiled and was gone.

Barry and Gerald wandered home. There seemed nothing more they could do, and both were still shaken up.

As they walked up the garden path, the front door flew open. The boys' grandfather stood there, waving his arms in the air. 'I'VE JUST SEEN YOU BOTH ON T.V!' he gasped. 'WHAT WERE YOU DOING, BREAKING INTO A JEWELLERY SHOP?'

'Breaking into a jewellery shop?' the boys echoed faintly.

'I'm getting the evening newspaper,' the old man was trembling, 'this is ridiculous!'

He picked up his walking stick from the hall. 'I'm not having this…' he wobbled his way down the garden path.

The boys stared after him, almost more shocked than he was. 'It was the plain clothes detective,' Gerald gasped.

'Yes, we should have known,' Barry replied.

They stood by the front door, until their grandfather returned. 'Here you both are… on the front page too!' The old man's face was white, as he held the newspaper up.

## DO YOU KNOW THESE TWO YOUTHS? IF SO CONTACT POLICE IMMEDIATELY.

*It is believed they broke into Jarvis Jewellers today, and stole jewellery worth thousands!*
*Mr Jarvis says they'll be offering a large reward for any information leading to arrests…*

Barry looked at Gerald, then at their grandfather. 'We're catching those men tonight! Don't worry grandad… we'll catch them.'

Gerald nodded his head. 'We'll get them this time, granda!' And the boys were off before their grandfather could stop them.

'We'll go to where the van was parked,' Barry said.

'What if they've moved it?' Gerald asked.

'We'll search the town,' Barry replied, grinning.

Gerald nodded, 'O.K. They might change their number plate...'

'We want to catch them, before they do!' Barry grinned again, though he didn't feel happy.

The boys returned home, exhausted and very discouraged! Their grandfather hugged them both. 'Good,' he said, 'you're just in time for supper.'

As they were having supper, the phone rang. Their grandfather answered it. 'Yes, the boys are here... you'll call tonight, you say... alright, sir.'

'Police,' he said, as Barry and Gerald exchanged glances, 'but no need to worry... none at all!'

Ten minutes later, the sergeant and one of his senior officers called at their house. The sergeant said, 'We want to thank you boys for taking the van's number. The three men were caught this afternoon, trying to leave the town. The jewellery was recovered – inside two of Jarvis's carrier bags, on the back seat. I've confirmed with Mr Jarvis, that you both will share their generous reward!'

'Well done, boys!' the old grandfather clapped his hands in

delight. Gerald and Barry stared at him – his face was pink as he winked back.

As soon as the sergeant and senior officer had gone, 'I've a confession to make,' their grandfather said. 'I found the van's number in your train-spotting notebook, Barry. I guessed what it was to do with, took a chance, and phoned the police!' The boys gasped and hugged the old man.

'This calls for a celebration,' their grandfather said. 'Twenty pounds each, and we're going out for a slap-up lunch tomorrow.'

The boys also received a generous reward each, from Mr Jarvis, the jeweller – and they treated their grandfather to a holiday by the seaside.

IF A BAD THING HAPPENS AND YOU USE YOUR HEAD – OUT OF THE BAD, MAY COME GOOD INSTEAD!

# BLIND PAINTER

In Southend, there was a man who was a brilliant painter. His name was Daniel Mantle, and he had been blind from birth. So how could he possibly paint his paintings, when he had never seen the world, with all its many colours?

He surely depended on others to describe scenes and then he internalised the information, adding his own personal, instinctive touch, style, colour and movement. He was lucky in that there was Caroline, his wife, and Angela, his daughter, who were always willing to describe scenes when they were there... but Daniel also painted when they were working!

Daniel had a gift that was almost unbelievable in its uniqueness – he painted by what he called his *internal vision* – and he also had a guide dog, who guided him in so many ways! Not only guiding him when outside, but sniffing out the paints for him as well. How this was, Daniel himself didn't know – after all, dogs were colour-blind weren't they? Or so it was thought, and proved by many scientists. Though no one had actually heard it from a dog!

And because Daniel was blind, and dogs were accepted as being colour-blind, many people said it was a *scam* – Daniel must be able to see, or someone else painted his pictures for him! Some of the authorities also didn't believe Daniel's gift was genuine, and he was told he had to have his eyes tested for blindness.

His wife, Caroline said he had already had tests and been registered blind. She said, 'I have the paperwork to prove it,' but still the authorities wouldn't believe it, and arranged for Daniel to go and see a specialist optician in London. Daniel and his wife were not happy about this, but they had to agree to it.

When they got to the appointment, Daniel was confronted by three specialists, who were drawn in by his claim to *Internal Vision* and *Help from a guide dog!* The fact that Daniel's paintings sold for enormous sums, had also added to the interest being shown.

Daniel's head and eyes were examined. He was given paints and paper, and obliged the specialists by producing a picture for them. The three finally agreed that, yes, Daniel was *blind* but had also an *Internal Vision* gift!

The result of his London visit, leaked out to the press. Shortly after their visit, a note was pushed through the letterbox: *If you don't put your paintings in your drive tonight, your wife and daughter will suffer.*

This was something Daniel had dreaded. 'I'm doing as they ask,' he told Caroline. 'I'm not having threats like that to my family. They can take the paintings!'

'No!' Caroline cried. 'We're not giving in to these idiots! Leave a message saying: *NO WAY! WE DON'T DEAL WITH CRIMINALS!*

I'm phoning the police.'

The police promised they'd be watching the drive, and perhaps Daniel could put some blank canvases there instead. They would need to be well wrapped up!

Daniel did as the police suggested. Then they waited for the blackmailers to turn up.

It was nearly five in the morning, and there was still no sign of them. 'I don't think they'll come now. Perhaps they've seen the police, and are scared,' Angela said. She turned away from the window, just seconds before bullets whistled through the glass.

'That's them all right!' Caroline hissed. 'We'll go out of the back door.'

'You and Angela do that,' Daniel said, 'but I'm phoning the police again. They told us they'd be here!'

A police car drove up, as he spoke.

'Though I've a feeling that won't be the end of the matter,' Caroline sighed.

She was right. The newspapers were full of headlines about paintings worth millions being sold – all the work of the famous blind painter, Daniel Mantle.

'We'll put a notice in the newspapers saying: *Unless, the paintings are recognised by the blind painter's guide dog – the paintings are fakes!*' Daniel exclaimed. 'Blind people have their own faithful dogs, and mine is exceptional in the way he helps me with my work.'

The newspapers were soon buzzing: **HOW COULD A GUIDE DOG IDENTIFY A PAINTING?** Daniel was invited to a television art programme. One of his most famous paintings was produced, with two other identical copies. The elite art world was holding its breath! Daniel wasn't allowed to even pat his dog or speak to him. *But without hesitation, the guide dog knew Daniel's painting, from the fakes!*

Two more of Daniel's paintings appeared, plus four fake copies. And again, the guide dog sorted them out. 'There's obviously more in this than mere smell – these paintings have been carefully cleaned,' the interviewer said. 'And the copies have similar texture, and colours.

I think we must acknowledge that Daniel Mantle is a brilliant blind painter, and accept what he says – he is helped by his guide dog!'

Shortly after his television appearance, the criminals appeared on the doorstep of the family home, claiming to be art dealers. They forced their way past Caroline – but that was as far as they got!

In seconds, they were prostrate on the floor, their guns grabbed and guarded by a noisily barking **guard** dog. They struggled to their feet, snatched the nearest painting, and were gone. 'Thank goodness you're alright, Caroline,' Daniel hugged his wife. Then he hugged his faithful dog – having proved to be both **guard** and **guide** dog. 'I don't care if they took my painting, perhaps they'll leave us alone at last!'

'It was a **fake**,' Caroline said, smiling. 'I thought they'd be back, so I did an exchange to trick them.'

The criminals were caught later, trying to flog the fake painting. And it is finally accepted by the art world: DANIEL MANTLE IS A BRILLIANT PAINTER WITH INTERNAL VISION. HIS GUIDE DOG HELPS HIM TO PAINT.

AND FAKES WILL ALWAYS BE SORTED OUT IN THE END!

# DOG AND CAT

In Manchester, there was a man whose name was Sam. He lived on his own in a little flat, with his dog called Toffee, and his cat called Taffy.

Toffee and Taffy wouldn't play with their toys – though they each had plenty of all descriptions, teddies, bells in balls, bones, rings, rubber fish and mice – some of them quite costly; but Toffee and Taffy just sat in their baskets, looking bored. They didn't want to eat much either. Sam took Toffee for walks, but it seemed he missed Taffy – he couldn't wait to get home, which is unusual for a dog!

One day, Sam was watching a dog program with his dog and cat. Toffee's eyes were shining, and Sam wondered if he could do any of the things that were being shown on the TV. He thought about it, and thought about it, and managed to get a book on **Dog Tricks**. Then he started to train Toffee – and after a while his dog managed to do the very same tricks!

All was going well, when Toffee suddenly decided to stop, and nothing would persuade him to do another trick...

instead he kept looking at Taffy, but she turned away! *Did he expect her to do dog tricks too?*

Sam decided he would try to teach her the same tricks, but it didn't really work… it seemed her heart wasn't in it. She jumped into Toffee's dog basket instead.

And strangely, when he played **fetch the ball** with Toffee, in the garden, Toffee took his time – was his dog ill or bored? Sam decided instead, he'd take Toffee out for a walk, and he would buy a lead for Taffy – there was no reason why she shouldn't come with them.

He bought her a bright pink lead. Toffee looked happy, but it didn't seem to appeal to Taffy… maybe she didn't like pink?

Suddenly, Sam felt desperate! Was Taffy the problem with Toffee? Perhaps he should give Taffy away – or if no one he knew wanted a cat, he could sell her. He looked down, and noticed how Toffee and Taffy had cuddled up together… Then Taffy turned and looked up at him.

No, he would never sell Taffy! How could he think of such a dreadful thing! 'It's alright, Taffy! It's alright,' he said aloud – and she brushed her fur against him, purring softly.

**But by now, Sam was worn out with stress!**

He couldn't stop thinking … about how to make both his pets happy…

And the next day, he was still **thinking** about it in the garden – when he suddenly fell over. He never even knew an ambulance had taken him to hospital.

When he came to, he found he was in an A&E ward, and

a nurse was saying, 'Thank goodness, I was wondering… now what would you like for your breakfast?'

'I want to go home,' Sam replied. 'I don't want breakfast here, I have to go home. My poor dog and cat! Toffee and Taffy must be famished.'

'We can't worry about your pets,' the nurse said briskly, trying to sound patient, 'it's **you** we've got to get strong again!'

'I AM STRONG AGAIN!' Sam managed to shout.

'Shhh… Shhh… Have you got a wife or children we could phone up? Perhaps they could collect you, after you've had your breakfast.' This patient was really hard work – she couldn't stay all day arguing.

'Yes! I've got Toffee and Taffy…' Sam began.

'But you said they were **animals**,' the nurse snapped. 'Anyway, I'll order your breakfast – tomato juice, cereal, egg and toast. Just eat it, when it comes and you'll soon be fit again!'

She hurried out of his cubicle and told the sister on duty, *'that man needs a psychologist etc. etc.'* But the odd thing was… when Sam's breakfast came, HE HAD GONE!

## HOW? WHO? WHAT? WHERE?

Yes, Toffee pushed him home in a wheelchair, where Taffy was waiting with a nice cup of tea. Before long, Toffee brought in a meal of tomato juice, cereal, and egg on toast. Then after the meal, Taffy brought him his favourite Americano coffee.

By the time he'd drunk his coffee, Sam felt so much better, he got out of the wheelchair, and they all three went off, for a pleasant walk together!

NOW, SHOULD YOUR DOG AND CAT MOPE ALL DAY, THEY TOO MIGHT NEED FUN IN THEIR OWN **SPECIAL** WAY… YOU ALSO COULD BE ASTONISHED TO FIND, JUST WHAT GOES ON INSIDE **THEIR** MIND! I mean some might love to shake a boot, while others would rather play the flute. Whatever they long for, **ALL DAY AND NIGHT**, you must be sure to get it **RIGHT!**

# Robots

Sir Higson Barnacle had a grand-sounding name, particularly now he'd been knighted for his thoroughly **original** machines, which managed to instantly dispose of all the employees in a giant-sized firm! Instead, the work would be done by his robots, and only the big boss would remain. Then all, the big boss would have to do, was press buttons…

However, when Higson retired, he began to regret his *magnificent-labour-intensive-saving* **original** *invention* more and more each day… which was already a year and two days. For 367 times in his adult life, he now realised what it was to have **NO** job, which, in his case, meant *NOTHING to do!*

Most married men, when they retire, soon find themselves busy, washing dishes, cleaning carpets, mending the garden fence, cutting the lawn (if it isn't shingle), carrying heavy shopping, and so on, and so on. But the housekeeper, cleaner, gardener, chauffeur and handyman did all of that. Though his wife was **very capable**, and would take over on their holidays. (And she always did the ironing, as no one was very keen or good at that!)

Poor Higson felt **bored** out of his giant-sized mind! In other words, he had **NOTHING** to do all day, as mentioned earlier. His wife was very sensible and was on the committee, or chairman, of every local lady's group. She also took women's keep fit classes, held cookery classes and organised bazaars! She had what one might call, a *dynamic personality* – she'd never quite approved of Higson's robots, as she liked doing **EVERYTHING HERSELF** – or rather, telling others what to do!

Higson had never wanted to do any of the domestic jobs other retired men did. He'd been far too busy, in his working life, inventing labour-saving devices. Then finally, a year before he retired, his highly intelligent robots *'took off'*! Overnight, they were the talk of every TV station, and by the next day, employees were being sacked world-wide, and his robots were being employed instead.

From being comfortably well-off, Higson was suddenly a millionaire, and then a **billionaire**. No financially-focused big boss wanted to pay for human labour, when robots (with high IQs) could do the work as well, if not better. After all, they **never** made a mistake as long as the boss didn't make one – and he **never** did!

What was the outcome of this happy event for Higson? It wasn't a HAPPY one at all. Poor Higson… he now had *far too much money!* Where was the challenge in life? There wasn't one! And worse still, he now had **NOTHING TO DO!**

He'd just had a bad cold, was still coughing and sneezing as he read the newspapers for the umpteenth time when his wife said, 'Higson, darling, why don't you join the local Bowling Club. I've heard from Mrs Glossop that they're terribly friendly there!' 'Yes,' Higson murmured, without listening. 'What did you say, dear?' 'You'd better go and enrol at the local Bowling Club tomorrow,' his wife said patiently.

Higson nodded absent-mindedly, 'Yes, I'm not sure...' He didn't finish what he was going to say. He'd suddenly pictured himself as Champion Bowler of the Highborough Bowling Club!

Next morning, he presented himself outside the locked door, at ten o'clock sharp. 'Any self-respecting bowling club should be open,' he thought irritably. 'Inefficiency... now if they had one of my robots...'

He was about to walk smartly home, when an elderly man opened the door.

'Yes,' he said peering round it, 'we welcome newcomers here. How much experience have you had?'

Higson hadn't had any experience, but he wouldn't admit that. 'A lot,' he replied, with a genial smile.

'Then you won't need to come to the roll-up! I'll enrol you straight away. I'm the club's secretary.'

Higson paid his £100 membership fee, and was now a fully-fledged member of Highborough Bowling Club. And he was in luck again!

There was a game about to start, and they were one short. He was asked to join in.

But Higson's good luck suddenly did a lurch. It was the first ball he'd ever bowled… in his life, apart from cricket. He picked up the ball and stood on the mat, thinking 'this is child's play!' He bent to roll it, but somehow it went wide… so wide it sailed over the bowling club wall. And there was a horrible noise of **shattered glass…**

Everyone stared at Higson, who had turned as white as his well-ironed shirt.

Before anyone said anything, a man's furious face appeared over the wall. 'Are you trying to be funny?' he asked, glaring at them all and Higson in particular!

Higson walked over, with a genial smile on his face. He took out a massive wodge of bank notes – and five minutes later, the bowling game was resumed at a comfortable pace… But now, without Higson, who'd excused himself and had gone home.

His wife was busy ironing his shirts. 'Did you have a good game, darling?' she asked.

'Brilliant!' Higson murmured.

'Will you be in the team?' she asked.

But he'd gone into the dining room to get a stiff drink.

His wife, smelling whiskey, said 'Here's the local newspaper dear. Why don't you go to the Writers Group, at the library? It might be more your line?'

Higson thought about it for a second. Then just to please her he asked, 'Which night is it, dear?'

'It's tonight,' she said briskly. 'We'll have supper early and you'd better take a notebook with you.'

The group was in full swing, when he walked in. They scarcely noticed him, as one member read aloud. Everyone made appreciative comments after the reading – except Higson. He hadn't understood a word of it! But then he was new, wasn't he? He'd better try to be humble… not like at the bowling club…

'Perhaps you could write something on the same lines, Mr…' the woman in charge suggested.
'Higson Barnacle,' he said with a genial smile. Then he

hissed to the man next door, *'What's the subject? Do you know?'*

'How you'd feel if you lost your job,' the man replied.

Higson stared back in shock. 'How do you mean?'

'Say a robot took over, and you had no work, no pay… no food,' the man explained impatiently.

Higson suddenly felt sick. Then he pulled himself together and began writing.

Half-a-dozen members read aloud their carefully-worded pieces, and now it was his turn. Higson stood up, cleared his throat and began, 'I would simply say, **'GREAT!'** Then I would simply **CELEBRATE!** Then I would simply get **A BETTER JOB!** Only those who dislike a **CHALLENGE** let such simple matters get them down. They should be **ASHAMED** of themselves…' he stopped, suddenly aware that all eyes were focused on him in **utter HORROR!**

*'Are you JOKING?'* one woman asked, gazing at him.

*'That is the **most awful CRAP** I've heard in **years**…'* another put in.

'Not what you would **DO** – but what you'd **FEEL?'** the group leader patiently explained. *'What would your* **FEELINGS** *be?'* **'He obviously hasn't got ANY!'** his neighbour said eyeing Higson glassily.

Then everyone else nodded, eyeing him even more glassily. Higson stared back and said, 'I don't think I'm feeling very well.'

They ignored him, as he hurried out of the Writers Group.

When he got home his wife asked 'How did you get on at the Writers Group darling?'

'It was simply GREAT!' Higson murmured.

'Perhaps you'll write a best seller soon,' his wife suggested. But he'd hurried into the dining-room to get a stiff drink.

Sadly, it seemed as if the Writers Group predictions would all come true – he felt simply at **rock bottom** himself, without any job!

BUT THE NEXT DAY, he knew exactly what he would do. He went into his science laboratory and produced a **newer** version of his **original** ROBOT … he pressed various buttons… did this and that…

Within the month, the latest models were ready to be

distributed world-wide. And that's when **EVERYTHING WENT WRONG!**

This ROBOT refused to obey instructions from the boss… it went wild, hurling other ROBOTS into the air… In other words, it simply caused utter and complete **CHAOS AND MAYHEM!**

Higson immediately agreed to withdraw the new model, and every previous ROBOT. After all, they might all go off the rails too! They might even throw the boss about!

Higson also agreed, without a murmur, to pay heavy compensation sums to all employees who had lost their jobs, and smaller compensation sums to all the bosses, who had lost their robots.

Then suddenly he felt happy for the first time in his life, ever since he was a penniless school boy.

But his wife was near to tears and cried, 'What on earth will you do? All your hard work has been destroyed, all because of that new model… *what on earth will you do, darling?*'

'My dear,' he said, taking her in his arms, 'I'm going to write a Scientific Paper about TECHNOLOGICAL CAUSE AND PSYCHOLOGICAL EFFECT and then…' but he couldn't tell her what else he was going to do, it sounded rather unusual, even **highly** unlikely…

Why?

**THIS WAS WHAT HE DID!** Higson arranged for all the robots to be collected worldwide, and returned to him. After that, under his inspired artistic supervision, he had them made into the **MOST MAGNIFICENT GIGANTIC CONTEMPORARY ART DISPLAY!** His Art Display was dropped in the middle of the sea, at what you might call, a **VERY** STRATEGIC SPOT and entitled:

## ROBOT MAKES PEACE WITH MAN

If anyone tried to destroy it – a robot would simply fly out of the sea and hug him. (Sometimes thousands might be flying to hug, at the same time!) Then they would, through magnetism, return to their **GIGANTIC** contemporary art display.

There are many differing opinions about Higson's contemporary art work… but then there always are, aren't there?

And although he is no longer a billionaire, not even a millionaire (being a very controversial *benefactor-entrepreneur*) he and his wife are well enough off to keep their domestic staff. His wife continues her committee work, and as for Higson… he has been invited to chair a new Worldwide Organisation: **HELP OTHERS… HELPS YOU!**

And he is busy raising money through his novel works of contemporary art, which speak volumes – but not all can understand what they are saying!

# BOTTLE BREAKER

Have you ever heard about a bottle which was so strong, it was **unbreakable**… you couldn't crack it, squash it, bend or crumple it? And what was this bottle made of? Not even Harry, its owner knew!

Harry had owned this particular bottle for many years. In fact, for so many, he couldn't remember when or where it had come from! It was so handy, being used for so many different things, and yet, it hadn't chipped, cracked, or been broken… it was a quite amazing bottle.

Harry was a shy man, and after his mother died, he seldom went out. He grew into a shaky, sad old man. Then one day, when he knocked over his unbreakable bottle, he had an idea: he would hold a competition to see if anyone could break the bottle!

He put poster adverts up in shops, and said he would give anyone £50, if they could break the bottle. Each person would pay £1 to take part in the competition, and they would have three goes at a time for their pound. The bottle must be broken into bits, to win the £50, and the money collected would go to the local hospital.

The competition would be on a Sunday in the park, a neighbour would be the judge. Then the local councillor heard of it, phoned Harry, and said he would be there too.

Bank Holiday Sunday was finally decided on, it was a warm sunny day, and over sixty people turned up, wanting to have *a go!* They paid their pound, at the park's entrance, and then they joined Harry. The bottle was placed in the middle of the group, and the first man walked over with a great big hammer and said, 'This is a piece of cake!' He took an almighty swing at the bottle, but couldn't even squash it. He had his three goes and said, 'I will be back later with a bigger hammer that will break it!'

The next competitor was a very large woman. She thumped down on the bottle, singing loudly 'Bright and breezy... this is easy...' and nearly fell over – and again the bottle remained undamaged. There followed a queue of competitors, who tried to squeeze it, threw it at nearby rocks, battered it, or thumped it like the first man – it went on and on for about four hours; but after another thirty people had had their go, the bottle still remained unbroken, un-squashed, un-dented, unscratched, or damaged in any way at all!

Because of the wonderful response to the competition, Harry decided to continue it on the Bank Holiday Monday. He again had a great turn-out, and lots of people wanted another go at breaking the bottle.

But again, no one succeeded in their attempts. One man was so determined to break the bottle that he said, 'I'll get a large garden roller and go over the bottle with that. It is sure to break then!' Off he went, to get his large garden roller. He came back, pushing it and everyone watched, as he went over the bottle three times. And still he couldn't break it. 'I give up!' said the man. 'What's it made of, Harry?' Harry smiled, 'I don't even know – except that it is unbreakable!'

Well, it was getting later and later and Harry said, 'The competition is only open for another half-an-hour!' There was a rush to finally break the bottle, but no one succeeded in even scratching it. Then Harry turned to the crowd and asked, 'So what shall I do with this bottle?'

'We'll put it in a glass case in our town hall,' the councillor replied, smiling. 'We've heard the hospital is delighted with the money you've raised, and we've all had such a good time. Thank you, Harry and now I'm inviting you all to supper – and yes, it's in our town hall!'

Harry had made so many friends that weekend – and it was all because of his UNBREAKABLE BOTTLE! IT REMAINS ON SHOW AT THE LOCAL TOWN HALL TO THIS VERY DAY.

Somer Town Hall

PLEASE DO NOT TRY TO REACH BOTTLE
YOU WILL ONLY BREAK FRAME –
BUT YOU WILL NEVER BREAK BOTTLE

HARRY'S UNBREAKABLE BOTTLE

# MYSTERY SUITCASE

Jim's wife spotted the advert. 'It's just the job for you, Jim! I can see you in your posh suit, white collar, smart tie.'

Jim sighed. He was tired of applying for jobs and being told, 'As you don't have a degree…' or 'As you have no former experience in…' or 'We're really looking for someone younger…'

He sighed and asked, 'Where did you say that job is, dear?' 'It's down in Cornwall…' Nora began.

'**Cornwall!** It would cost a bomb to get there,' Jim replied.

'Don't you worry about the money,' Nora said patiently, desperate to keep his interest going. After all, it was a chance, wasn't it? No specific experience or qualifications were required, were they?

She read it out again, 'Gentleman… smartly dressed… ready to assume responsibility… pleasant manner…' It's **YOU**, Jim! I can see you in that job already.'

'Assume responsibility for **what?**' Jim asked. If it was a posh hotel, supermarket, or nuclear power plant… what chance had he?

She looked through the details. 'Well, it doesn't actually say **what…** but it's still the job for you, I have this feeling in my guts!' The feeling was passing a little, but Nora was trying hard.

'Oh alright,' he smiled. He'd do anything for her − even if it was his one thousandth interview! One more wouldn't really hurt, would it? 'I'd better write and ask for an interview.'

'I'll phone up,' Nora said quickly, thinking of his hand-writing. 'I'll say I'm your secretary, and you're busy seeing to clients.'

**'Seeing to clients?'** Jim echoed.

'Well, we've got to keep our end up somehow,' Nora said, trying not to snap, 'other people do!'

Jim's wife phoned up and he was given an interview in a week's time. She booked him into a posh hotel (it was always good to say where you were staying); she washed, ironed and packed his best shirt; folded and packed his best suit, tie, socks, etc. Then she suddenly cried, 'Jim, do wake up, dear! How will you travel there? We'll get you a train ticket!'

'Now look 'ere Nora, we're not millionaires − I'm going by coach,' Jim said firmly.

On the following Monday, she saw him onto the coach to Cornwall. He looked around him, wondering how many others would be applying for the same job as he was. There seemed to be about thirty very smart, very pleasant-looking, very efficient, **younger** men – and about half-a-dozen, mostly older women. But all those *younger* men… they'd be going to interviews, wouldn't they? Perhaps he should get on the return coach – and save the money of two nights in a posh hotel…

Jim was worn out with worrying, and fell asleep. He was woken some hours later, by the driver's voice, as the coach pulled into a motorway services. 'You'll all want to take a breather, stretch your legs, have something to eat, coffee, tea, etc. – there are good toilet facilities here.' Jim wasn't anxious to get out, but then he noticed an elderly woman with sticks; and when he stepped off the coach, the hatch was open as a buggy was hauled out. He walked over and helped the elderly woman – at least, he could still do something for others! Then he lingered… a young man in jeans and bright red tea shirt, was looking for his suitcase. Jim thought, 'that's the way **NOT** to dress for an interview – not if one wanted the job!'

After a coffee and sandwich, Jim was back on the coach for the final lap of the journey. He instantly fell asleep, and was amazed in the change of scenery, when he opened his eyes in Cornwall!

The coach was parking near a large, impressive hotel. This

was his destination, and already the smart younger men were standing up, ready to leave.

Jim's legs were stiff but he tried to assume an **air of responsibility**, as he climbed off the coach, tipped the driver and entered the hotel. One never knew if there might be spies watching… he shook himself. 'Take a grip, man!' he nearly said it aloud. 'This is real, **not** a comedy play!'

He picked up his door key at reception, and his room was pointed out on a map of the hotel interior. 'There's a lift over there, sir,' the young woman said helpfully. *Oh dear, did he look that old!* 'I'll walk,' he mumbled and tried to smile pleasantly.

He eventually found his room having forgotten which the direct route was, apart from the lift. His one suitcase had not yet arrived, but as it looked shabby… no, it wasn't! Nora had bought him a *new* one for the occasion… At any rate, it wasn't outside yet; but then he was on the fourth floor – perhaps they worked from bottom, up…

Jim flung himself on the luxurious bed, and fell fast asleep. He woke up two hours later. *Where was he? Which day was it? Why on earth was he here?* He was here for that interview…

Then he remembered about his suitcase…

He climbed off the bed and hurried over to the door.

There was a **suitcase** there alright – **A JAZZY RED ONE WHICH DEFINITELY WASN'T HIS!**

He immediately lifted the receiver by his bed. 'You've given me the **WRONG** suitcase,' he tried to keep calm. 'It **DEFINITELY** isn't **MINE!** Please collect it **IMMEDIATELY** and **SORT THE MATTER OUT!'**

'I'm sorry sir, our porter is off duty,' a voice said politely. 'Perhaps you could check the label – we rarely make mistakes here – you may have misread it or…'

'I know what I'm **SEEING!** Alright, I'll check again,' Jim tried to relax a little, '**BUT** I'm not happy about this!' He put the receiver back, and walked determinedly to the door. He opened the door, and peered at the label on the suitcase. It was written by Nora… the very same label she'd attached to **HIS** suitcase, was attached to this **JAZZY SUITCASE!**

He couldn't believe it and began to think he was seeing things – **OR** had Nora tied it to the **WRONG** suitcase by mistake… but it wasn't his scruffy old suitcase either. He hadn't bought a suitcase like this one, **NOT EVER, not EVEN WANTED TO!**

The suitcase wasn't locked. He pulled out the contents and

stared at them in shock… **JEANS! RED TEA SHIRTS! TRAINERS!**

Someone was playing a **TRICK** on him – a not very funny one! No, it was **DARN AWFUL!** And the **RED** tea shirts rang a distant bell in his mind – WHERE HAD HE SEEN ONE LIKE THAT? **The fellow who stood by the hatch at the motorway services stop!**

Nora would be **SO DISAPPOINTED**, after all the effort they'd made; or, rather, she'd made – what on **EARTH** should he do?

Then Jim tried to see the funny side of it! At least, the clothes were obviously brand new and clean, whereas the suit he'd travelled in was crumpled, and his white shirt distinctly dirty, round the collar!

Jim told himself it didn't really matter… it was all rather a joke… yes, a very funny joke…

But Nora's anxious face kept coming into his mind. He pictured her ironing his best shirt, folding his best suit… all the trouble she'd taken! And they both would like living in Cornwall… they needed a change from Birmingham…

SOMEHOW, HE HAD TO GET HIS SUITCASE BACK! AND **BEFORE** THE INTERVIEW!

When he went down for his evening dinner, he eyed the other visitors closely. He tried to visualise them wearing **jazzy clothes!** And they stared back at him…

He pushed down the starter, main course and pudding – then he had tea, instead of coffee – or he'd never sleep tonight… not with all that **SUITCASE MYSTERY** on his mind!

But he couldn't bring himself to put on the brand new, pillar-box red pyjamas, he found in the suitcase. And he stared blankly at the hair cream, hair lotion, hairspray… underarm this, that and the other… there was even something for the face, besides after-shave lotion… and sun creams… Then there was a bottle of what was it… *male perfume?*

He didn't bother washing, and climbed into bed in his, by now, grubby underwear. He thought he could smell it, and what was worse… he couldn't sleep a wink… then he had a **nightmare!** A *younger* man was wearing his new suit, his white shirt, carefully polished shoes…

Jim woke late… hesitated, but only for a second… before putting on brand new jeans and red tea shirt, with matching red socks, and white trainers. He caught the lift downstairs, gobbled his cereal and coffee, and tried to think about the interview, details of which he could only vaguely remember.

Then he climbed into a taxi that drew up outside the front porch. Was it for somebody else? He didn't know. He scarcely knew what he was doing!

And the driver was staring at him… he asked where Jim wanted to go. Jim tried to tell him, but it came out in a funny high voice, and the driver stared even harder… then they were off!

They arrived at the gates of a HUGE STATELY HOME… what was the man's name? Jim felt panicky. Had Nora mentioned it, or only the address? He could only think of *branding* something – that couldn't be right, could it?

Still feeling sick and shaky, the taxi deposited him at the front door, and he paid the driver. 'Cheer up,' the driver said, with a friendly smile, 'I've heard they EAT folks here – but they never dress up like you!'

The front door opened before Jim had even pressed the bell.

'Come in,' a young woman said, 'our manager, Mr Brandish is waiting for you!'

But just as Jim walked into the stately home, a red sports car drove up, and a young man jumped out… wearing *HIS* **NEW SUIT, SHIRT and TIE!**

Jim felt boiling hot, then icy cold. He thought he was going to pass out with shock, as Mr Brandish stepped forward and shook the new arrival by the hand. 'Yes,' he said, 'I'm ready to interview you. What sort of a journey did you have?'

Jim stood awkwardly in the vast hall, and looked at portraits of ancestors. They seemed a surprisingly genial lot, considering the look of the manager! He was tall, thin, with a narrow face, hard mouth, and as for his eyes…

'What did you think of him?' a voice asked.

Did the old man mean the **manager** or the portrait – taken by surprise Jim muttered, 'He looks very nice to me…'

'And who are you?' the old man asked.

Jim tried to gather his wits. 'Jim Larkin,' he cleared his throat, 'I've come for an interview here.'

'Ah yes,' the old man said thoughtfully. 'I'm Lord Chartley, tenth Baron – I'm glad you like my ancestor. That's a good start, and since my manager is interviewing everyone else… I think I'd like to interview you. Let's take a walk outside – so stuffy in here, isn't it?'

Jim smiled and took the old man's arm.

Then Lord Chartley said, 'So glad you haven't come in

those DREADFUL CLOTHES! I can't stand all that formal stuff. Do you like animals?'

'Oh yes,' Jim replied. He didn't know much about animals, but he liked what he'd seen of them.

'We'll go and visit the chimps first. There's one who's nearly as old as me.'

And after that it was a **forgone conclusion** as to what was what!

The chimp hugged Jim as if they were old friends.

'I can see Brandy has taken to you… he doesn't take to everyone… not those starchy young men in managerial clothes! But I knew… I knew…'

Horses and donkeys took to Jim too – so did some cows, and sheep with lambs!

Perhaps they sensed what he'd been through; whatever it was, he had a natural way with animals.

Finally, as they walked back to the house, Lord Chartley turned to Jim and said, 'You're the man to take over from Mr Brandish. I never could STAND that man… and now he's retiring, he's looking for a carbon copy of himself when he was younger!'

Jim smiled and silently agreed.

'Now you're the hands-on, friendly sort of gentle type – don't mind getting your cuffs dirty. That's what we need here. I'm offering you the job right away – no time to waste, you know!'

'Thank you, Lord Chartley,' Jim smiled, 'I'm **very happy indeed** to take it.' And he never spoke a truer word!

When he returned to the hotel, Jim took off the borrowed clothes and replaced them in the suitcase. He put on his own suit, shirt, tie and shoes, and he left the case at reception on his way out. He spent the rest of the day in Truro, and caught an overnight coach back. He couldn't wait to get home!

He telephoned Nora on his arrival in Birmingham. She was standing at their garden gate waiting for him. 'How did you get on?' she asked, hugging him.

*'I got it!'* he told her.

**Oh! Oh! Oh!** They were both dancing for joy… then by the front door, he saw his suitcase!

'I never thought you would,' Nora said. 'I mean you only had your travel suit on didn't you…'

Jim was busy opening the suitcase. He read the note inside: *Sorry about mistake. Had to change lock, but here's new key. I'm going to an interview for a barman here in Birmingham – the job will suit me much better. Good luck and thanks.*

*P.S. I've put in two red tea shirts. I think the chimp likes red. He never hugged me.*

The signature was unreadable – but the **MYSTERY** was solved!